獻給幫助我找到書的Justin Chanda

作者／黛比‧里帕斯‧奧伊（Debbie Ridpath Ohi）

童書作家及繪者，她曾與Simon & Schuster、HarperCollins、Random House、Little Brown、Stone Bridge Press 和 Writer's Digest等出版社合作，並為作家麥可‧伊恩‧布萊克（Michael Ian Black）《我的情緒認知繪本4部曲》、《光屁屁小超人》（野人文化出版）繪製插畫。
官網：DebbieOhi.com / Twitter: @inkyelbows / Instagram: @inkygirl.

小野人 44
誰偷走了我的書？【中英雙語繪本】

作　者　黛比‧里帕斯‧奧伊（Debbie Ridpath Ohi）

野人文化股份有限公司
社　　長　張瑩瑩
總 編 輯　蔡麗真
主　　編　陳瑾璇
責任編輯　李怡庭
行銷企劃經理　林麗紅
行銷企畫　蔡逸萱、李映柔
封面設計　周家瑤
內頁排版　洪素貞

讀書共和國出版集團
社　　長　郭重興
發行人兼出版總監　曾大福
業務平臺總經理　李雪麗
業務平臺副總經理　李復民
實體通路組　林詩富、陳志峰、郭文弘、王文賓、賴佩瑜
網路暨海外通路組　張鑫峰、林裴瑤、范光杰
特販通路組　陳綺瑩、郭文龍
電子商務組　黃詩芸、李冠穎、林雅卿、高崇哲、吳眉姍
專案企劃組　蔡孟庭、盤惟心
閱讀社群組　黃志堅、羅文浩、盧煒婷
版 權 部　黃知涵
印 務 部　江域平、黃禮賢、林文義、李孟儒
出　　版　野人文化股份有限公司
發　　行　遠足文化事業股份有限公司
　　　　　地址：231 新北市新店區民權路 108-2 號 9 樓
　　　　　電話：（02）2218-1417　傳真：（02）8667-1065
　　　　　電子信箱：service@bookrep.com.tw
　　　　　網址：www.bookrep.com.tw
　　　　　郵撥帳號：19504465 遠足文化事業股份有限公司
　　　　　客服專線：0800-221-029
法律顧問　華洋法律事務所　蘇文生律師
印　　製　凱林彩印股份有限公司
初版首刷　2022 年 08 月

國家圖書館出版品預行編目(CIP)資料

誰偷走了我的書?/黛比‧里帕斯‧奧伊(Debbie Ridpath Ohi)作；野人文化編輯部譯. -- 初版. -- 新北市：野人文化股份有限公司出版：遠足文化事業股份有限公司發行，2022.08
　　面；　公分. -- (小野人；44)
中英對照
譯自：Where are my books?
ISBN 978-986-384-674-1(精裝)

874.599　　　　　　　　　　　110022347

Where Are My Books?
By Debbie Ridpath Ohi
Copyright © 2015 by Debbie Ridpath Ohi
Complex Chinese translation copyright © 2022 by Yeren Publishing House
Published by arrangement with Simon & Schuster Books for Young Readers, An imprint of Simon & Schuster Children's Publishing Division, and Curtis Brown, Ltd. through Bardon-Chinese Media Agency
All rights reserved

誰偷走了我的書？

野人文化
官方網頁

野人文化
讀者回函

線上讀者回函專用
QR CODE，你的寶貴意見，將是我們進步的最大動力。

WHERE
ARE MY
BOOKS?

誰偷走了我的書？

作者／黛比・里帕斯・奧伊
(Debbie Ridpath Ohi)

野人

Spencer **loved** books.
His favorite bedtime book was *Night-Night, Narwhal.*
Sometimes he read it aloud.

史賓賽熱愛書本。
他最喜歡的床邊故事書是《晚安，獨角鯨》，
有時候他會大聲唸出來。

Every night, Spencer put the book back where it belonged.
That way he'd always be able to find it.

每天晚上，史賓賽都會把書放回原本的地方，
這樣他下次就能立刻找到。

Until one morning . . .

直到某天早上……

「我的書跑到哪裡去了?」
"WHERE IS MY BOOK?"

史賓賽找遍**所有地方**,但還是沒找到。
Spencer looked **everywhere**,
but it was no use.

Night–Night, Narwhal was GONE.
《晚安,獨角鯨》不見了。

That evening, he chose *Tenacious Todd*.
It was okay.

那天晚上，他選了《堅強的陶德》來讀。
這個故事還不錯。

可是陶德是一隻蟾蜍，蟾蜍是兩棲類，
而關於兩棲類的書應該要在午餐後的故事時間讀才對。
But Todd was a toad, and toads were amphibians, and amphibian
books were supposed to be for right-after-lunch story time.

When Spencer woke the next morning, *Tenacious Todd* was **gone**.
當史賓賽隔天早上醒來時，《堅強的陶德》不見了。

Every morning, **another book was missing**.
每到早上，就會有另一本書失蹤。

Next to go was *Send in the Clown Fish.*

下一本不見的是《小丑魚進場》，

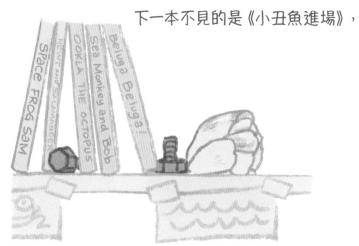

Then *Beluga Beluga!* vanished.

接著《白鯨，白鯨！》消失了。

Sea Monkey and Bob went missing.

《鮑伯與海猴子》也失蹤了。

Things were getting out of hand.

事情愈來愈不對勁。

Spencer vowed to find out what was going on.

史賓賽發誓要查出發生了什麼事。

His father did not know what happened
to *Night-Night, Narwhal.*

他的爸爸不知道《晚安，獨角鯨》到哪裡去了。

Spencer's mother had no idea either.
Nor had she seen *Tenacious Todd, Send in the Clown Fish,*
Beluga Beluga!, or any of Spencer's other missing books.

史賓賽的媽媽也不知道。
她也沒看到《堅強的陶德》、《小丑魚進場》、《白鯨，白鯨！》
或其他失蹤的書。

That left only ONE PERSON . . .
那麼就只剩下一個人了……

「我的書跑到哪裡去了？」

It was time for a new plan.

是時候換個新計畫了。

That night, Spencer set a trap with his copy of *Space Frog Sam*.

那天晚上，史賓賽用他的書《太空蛙山姆》做了一個陷阱。

The next morning . . .

隔天早上……

it was time for Spencer to get his books back!
史賓賽要去把他的書拿回來!

Spencer ran faster.
The thief was **just around the corner.**
史賓賽跑得更快了。
那個小偷就在附近。

"AHA!" he said. "That's my · · ·

「啊哈！」他說。「那是我的……」

"book?"

「書？」

Spencer didn't know squirrels like to read.

史賓賽不知道松鼠喜歡閱讀。

It gave him a great idea.

這讓他想到一個好點子。

史賓賽告訴松鼠他們可以借走他的書，
Spencer told the squirrels they could borrow his books.

但是要遵守幾條規則。
But there would be rules.

Just like at the library, they had to return the books
   they borrowed before they could borrow more.
就像在圖書館一樣，他們必須先把借走的書
還回來，才能再借更多書，

But they didn't need to leave anything behind.
不過他們不需要留下什麼作為交換。

Spencer even helped them
pick out their first book.
史賓賽甚至幫忙他們挑第一本書。

He chose one for himself, too.

他也幫自己選了一本。

And he promised to read it aloud.

而且他保證會大聲唸出來。